Esmerelda

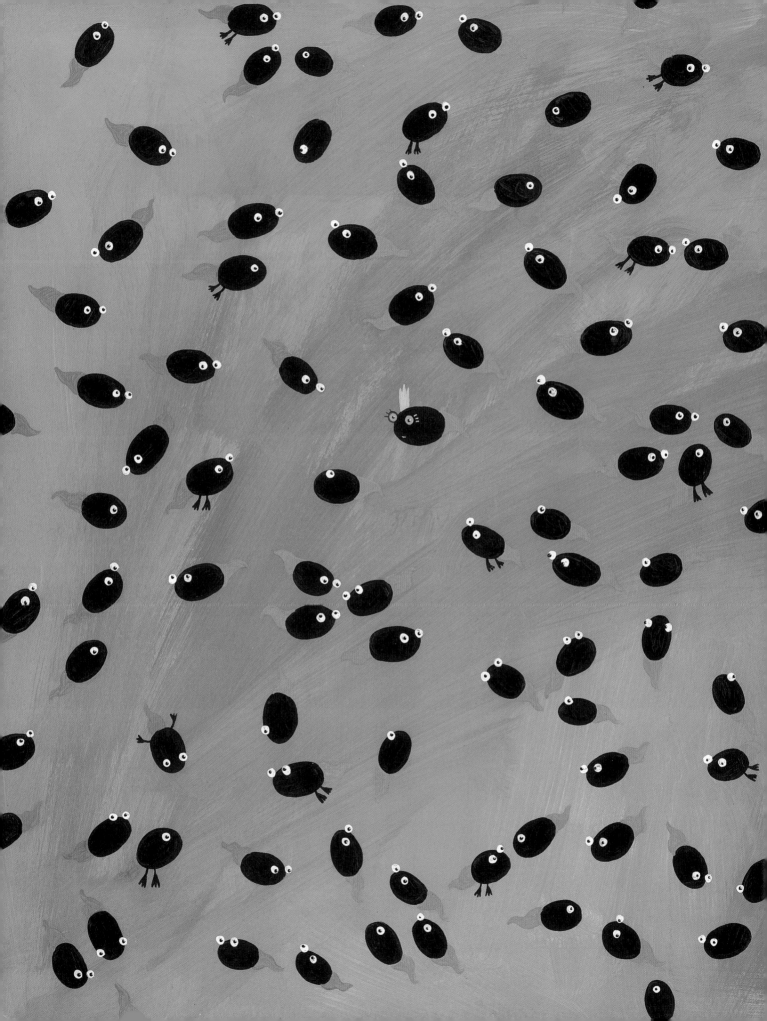

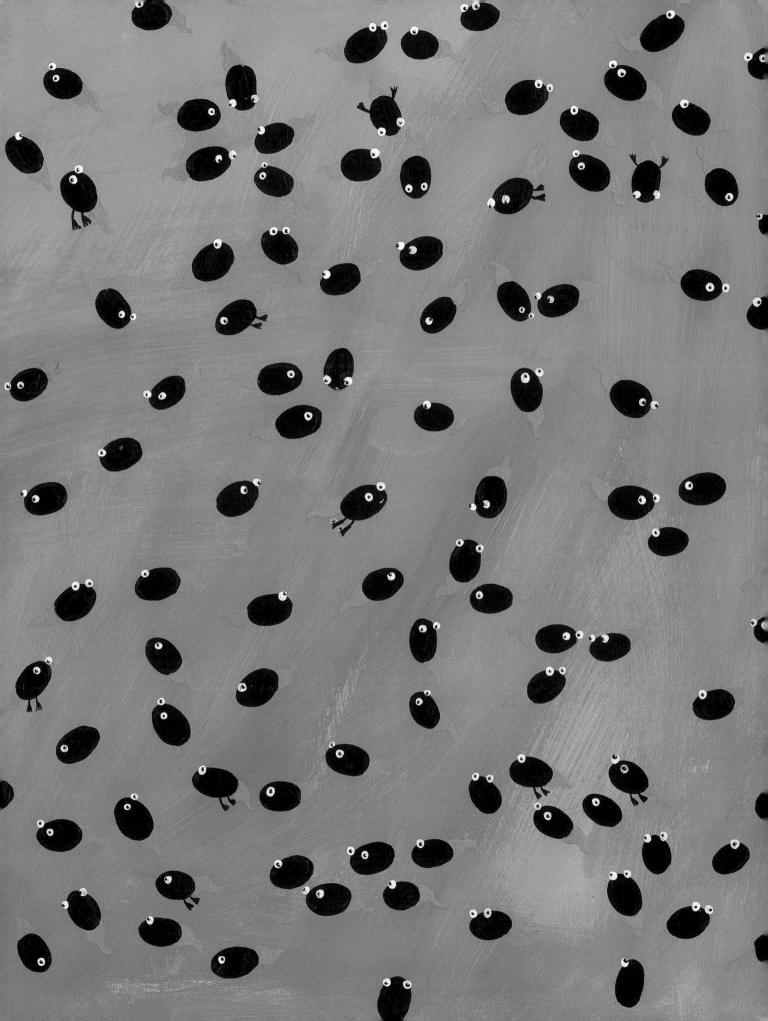

To Jenny with love – KW

For Aunt Mary, Aunt Rosaleen and Aunt Veronica – LM

First published 2000 by Macmillan Children's Books
This edition published 2001 by Macmillan Children's Books
a division of Macmillan Publishers Limited
20 New Wharf Road, London N1 9RR
Basingstoke and Oxford
Associated companies throughout the world
www.panmacmillan.com

ISBN 0 333 76051 4

Text copyright © Karen Wallace 2000
Illustrations copyright © Lydia Monks 2000

The right of Karen Wallace and Lydia Monks to be identified as the
author and illustrator of this work has been asserted by them in accordance
with the Copyright, Designs and Patents Act 1988.

5 7 9 8 6

A CIP catalogue record for this book is available
from the British Library.

Printed in China

Esmerelda

Story by
Karen Wallace

Illustrated by
Lydia Monks

MACMILLAN CHILDREN'S BOOKS

Esmerelda was a frog
who thought she was a princess.

She didn't like catching flies
like the other frogs. She didn't
like sitting in the mud and feeling
the sun on her back. And she hated
splashing in the pond even though
the water was warm and gooey.

Instead Esmerelda pushed her feet into satin slippers.

She **squeezed** her pale green tummy into a floaty white dress.

Then she pulled on the little gold crown Granny Spotted Frog had given her on her birthday.

"One day my prince will come," said Esmerelda to herself.

And she sat on her lily pad and waited.

On the other side of the pond lived a frog called Esmond.

Esmond was a frog who thought he was a prince.

He didn't like diving for beetles like the other frogs. He didn't like floating in the pond with his nose poking through the weed. And he hated hopping about in the reeds and jumping into the water with a splash.

Instead Esmond *pushed*
his skinny green arms into a fancy blue waistcoat.
He squeezed his webbed feet into long black boots.
And he buckled on the tiny silver sword Grandfather
Green Frog had given him for his birthday.

Then Esmond hid in the buttercups and read fairy stories.

He especially liked the one about the princess who kissed the frog and turned him into a prince.

"I'm worried about Esmerelda," said Mrs Spotted Frog to Mrs Green Frog. She waggled her back legs in the soft slimy mud. "She's not like other frogs."

Mrs Green Frog flicked out her long tongue and swallowed a fly. "I'm worried about Esmond," she said. "He's not like other frogs. He reads fairy stories."

"Esmerelda thinks she's a princess," said Mrs Spotted Frog in a low voice, hoping no one would hear her. "I'm sure it's not right."

But a pond is just like a village.
Everyone knows what everyone else is doing.

"Why shouldn't Esmerelda want to be a princess?"
croaked Grandmother Spotted Frog from behind the reeds.
"All young frogs should have dreams. Besides, she loves
the crown I gave her for her birthday."

"Why shouldn't Esmond want to be a prince?"
muttered Grandfather Green Frog from under a clump of
weed. "We don't all have to be the same. What's more, he
loves the fairy stories I gave him."

Mrs Spotted Frog and Mrs Green Frog pulled down their mouths and looked cross. They thought everybody should be exactly the same. That way there could be no nasty surprises and nobody would think anybody else was peculiar.

Mrs Spotted Frog and Mrs Green Frog were about to say something bad-tempered about old frogs giving young frogs ridiculous birthday presents and filling their heads full of silly ideas when a hungry heron flew over the pond.

And that
was the end of that.
Because there is no time
for disagreements when a
hungry heron is about.

Late that night, a wind blew up.
It ruffled the reeds at the edge of the pond.
It made ripples on the water.
It tugged at the lily pad where Esmerelda was asleep.

Rrrip!

The lily pad broke free
and floated over to the
other side of the pond.

Esmerelda smiled in her sleep.

She dreamed she was a princess sailing in a boat.

In his bed in the buttercups, Esmond
sat up and rubbed his eyes. The ripples in the
pond sparkled in the moonlight. Esmond imagined he
was a prince in his castle, looking out at the stars.

Then Esmond saw a little boat
sailing towards him.

He saw a little golden crown!
He saw a floaty white dress!

Esmond's heart went **bang**
in his chest.

He knew his princess
had found him at last!

Esmerelda woke up.
She had the strangest feeling
that something extraordinary
was about to happen.

Then she saw the tiny silver sword.
She saw the fancy blue waistcoat.
She saw the fine black boots.
She knew her prince had come at last.

Esmerelda
leapt off her lily pad.
Esmond threw open his arms.

Their lips
touched.

Only Granny Spotted Frog and Grandfather Green Frog saw Prince Esmond and Princess Esmerelda leave that night. A red carpet unrolled all the way to the buttercups. A crystal coach pulled by six white doves appeared beside the reeds.

The Prince and Princess flew into the black starry sky.

At the edge of the pond Grandfather Green Frog settled into the mud. "It's just like I said," he murmured to Granny Spotted Frog. "All young frogs should believe in fairy tales."

Granny Spotted Frog chuckled, "And sometimes dreams do come true!"